Just Like
Mummy

For my mummy,
who is the absolute best!

First published in the United Kingdom in 2018 by
Pavilion Children's Books
43 Great Ormond Street
London
WC1N 3HZ

An imprint of Pavilion Books Company Limited

Publisher and editor: Neil Dunnicliffe
Art director and designer: Lee-May Lim

Layout © Pavilion Children's Books, 2018
Text and illustrations © Lucy Freegard, 2018

The moral rights of the author and illustrator have been asserted

ISBN: 9781843653523

A CIP catalogue record for this book is available from the British Library.

10 9 8 7 6 5 4 3 2 1

Reproduction by ColourDepth, UK
Printed by To⬛⬛⬛⬛⬛ Ltd, China

This book can be ordered direc⬛⬛⬛⬛⬛⬛⬛e at www.pavilionbooks.com,

Just Like Mummy

Lucy Freegard

PAVILION

My friends say that when they grow up,
they want to be...

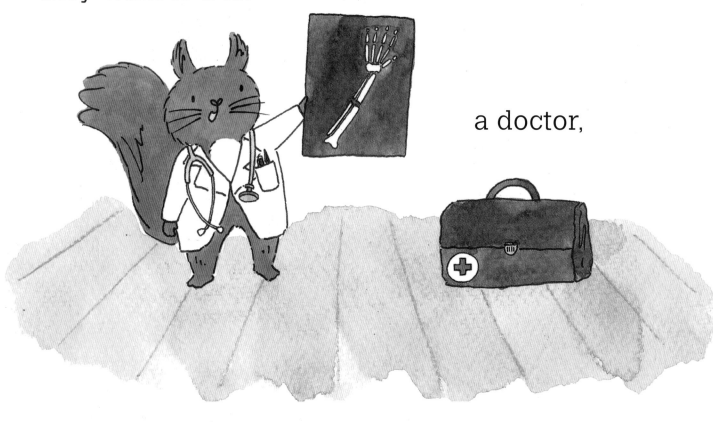

a doctor,

an astronaut,

and a firefighter.

But when I grow up, I want to be...

TOYS

...just like Mummy!

I will know so many
things about the earth,

the sea, and...

...the stars in the sky.

When I'm as grown up as Mummy,
I will be practical *and* creative.

I will know exactly
which notes to play.

And how to grow
my own food.

When I grow up,
I will have lots of adventures.

Mummy says there
are **fantastic** days...

...and **frustrating** days.

We get things wrong sometimes,

but we *always* find reasons to laugh!

Mummy says we all do things we regret.

Sometimes a **cuddle**
is all you need to feel better.

All my friends think Mummy is **awesome**,
especially at parties.

She's great at hiding treasure,

sharing ice cream
(most of the time),

and all kinds of joining in!

When I grow up,
I'm going to be
just like Mummy.

Because no matter how clever she seems...

...Mummy is always ready for fun,

just like me!